Diary of a Wombat

written by
Jackie French

illustrated by
Bruce Whatley

Angus&Robertson
An imprint of HarperCollins*Publishers*

Angus&Robertson
An imprint of HarperCollins*Publishers*, Australia

First published in Australia in 2002
This edition published in 2003
by HarperCollins*Publishers* Pty Limited
ABN 36 009 913 517
A member of the HarperCollins*Publishers* (Australia) Pty Limited Group
www.harpercollins.com.au

HarperCollins*Publishers*
25 Ryde Road, Pymble, Sydney, NSW 2073, Australia
31 View Road, Glenfield, Auckland 10, New Zealand
77-85 Fulham Palace Road, London W6 8JB, United Kingdom
2 Bloor Street East, 20th floor, Toronto, Ontario M4W 1A8, Canada
10 East 53rd Street, New York NY 10032, USA

National Library of Australia Cataloguing-in-Publication data:

French, Jackie.
    Diary of a wombat.
    For children.
    ISBN 0 207 19995 7 (hbk).
    ISBN 0 207 19836 5 (pbk.).
    1. Wombats - Juvenile literature. I. Whatley, Bruce. II. Title.
599.24

Bruce Whatley used acrylic paints to create the illustrations for this book
Cover and internal design by Lore Foye, HarperCollins Design Studio
Colour reproduction by Colourwize Studio, Adelaide, South Australia
Printed in China by Everbest Printing Co. Ltd on 128gsm Japanese Matt Art

24 23 22   09 10 11

To Mothball, and all the others.
JF

Thanks for letting me play, Jackie.
This was fun.
BW

Monday

Morning: Slept.

Afternoon: Slept.

Evening: Ate grass.

Scratched.

Night: Ate grass.

Slept.

Tuesday

Morning: Slept.

Afternoon: Slept.

Evening: Ate grass.

Night: Ate grass. Decided grass is boring.

Scratched. Hard to reach the itchy bits.

Slept.

Wednesday

Morning: Slept.

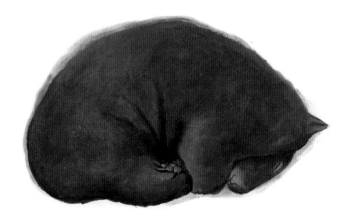

Afternoon: Mild cloudy day.

Found the perfect dustbath.

Discovered flat, hairy creature
invading my territory.

Fought major battle with
flat, hairy creature.

Won the battle.

Demanded a carrot.

The carrot was delicious.

Evening: Demanded more carrots.

No response.

Chewed hole in door.

FOR PETE'S SAKE,
GIVE HER SOME
CARROTS!

Ate carrots.

Scratched.

Went to sleep.

Thursday

Morning: Slept.

Afternoon:
Discovered the perfect scratching post.

Evening: Demanded carrots.
No response.
Tried yesterday's hole.
Curiously resistant to my paws.

Bashed up garbage bin
till carrots appeared.

Ate carrots.

Began new hole in soft dirt.

Went to sleep.

Friday

Morning: Slept.

Afternoon: Discovered new scratching post.

Also discovered a new
source of carrots.

Evening: Someone has filled in my new hole.

Soon dug it out again.

Night: Worked on hole.

Saturday

Morning: Moved into new hole.
Afternoon: Rained.

New hole filled up with water.
Moved back into old hole.

Evening: Discovered even more carrots.
Never knew there were so many carrots in the world.
Carrots delicious.

Night: Finished carrots.

Slept.

<u>Sunday</u> Morning: Slept.

Afternoon: Slept.

Evening: Slept.

Night: Offered carrots at the back door.

Why would I want carrots when I feel like rolled oats?
Demanded rolled oats instead. Humans failed
to understand my simple request.
Am constantly amazed how dumb humans can be.

Chewed up one pair of boots, three cardboard boxes,
eleven flower pots and a garden chair
till they got the message.

Ate rolled oats.

Scratched. Went to sleep.

Monday

Morning: Slept.

Afternoon: Felt energetic.
Wet things flapped against
my nose on my way to the back door.

Got rid of them.

Demanded oats AND carrots.
Only had to bash the garbage bin
for five minutes before they arrived.

Evening: Have decided that humans
are easily trained and make quite good pets.

Night: Dug new hole
to be closer to them.

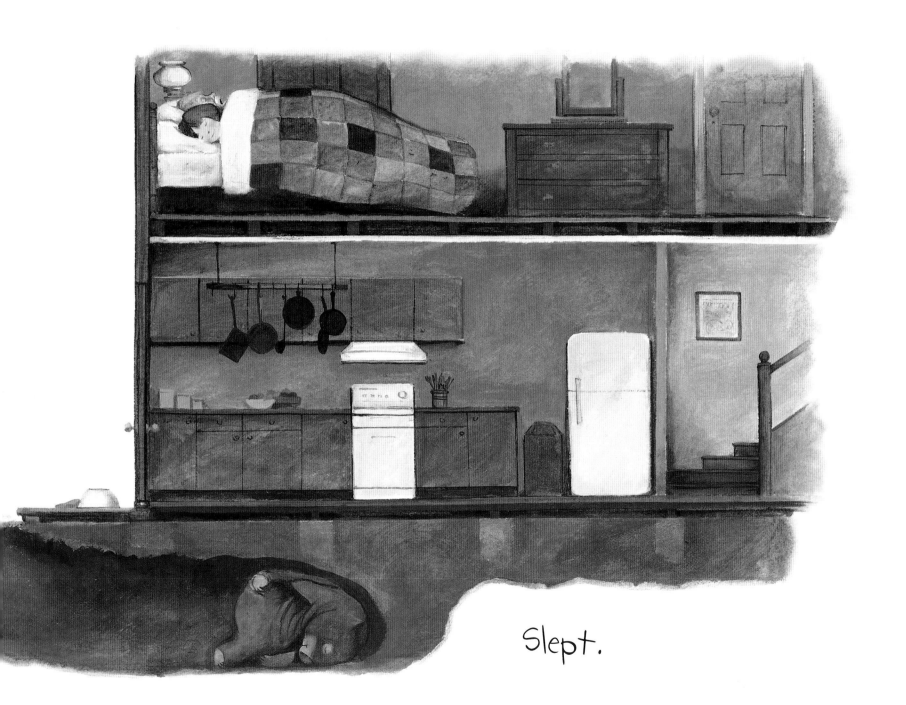

Slept.